This book is given with love

TO:

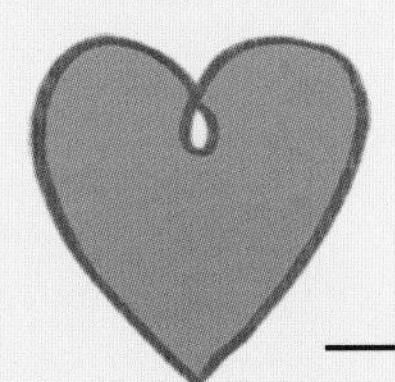

FROM:

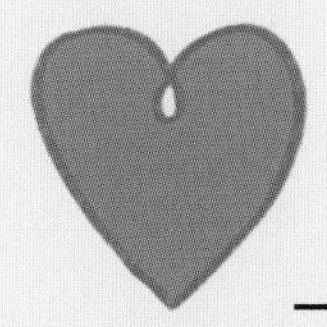

Published in the United States by Puppy Dogs & Ice Cream, Inc.
ISBN: 978-1-949474-66-4
Edition: June 2020

For all inquiries, please contact us at:
info@puppysmiles.org

To see more of our books, visit us at:
www.PuppyDogsAndIceCream.com

the Yeti is Ready

ROYCE KUNZE

Some words from the Himalayas

Himalayas - A range of mountains on the border of two countries: China and India. The Himalayas are home to the highest mountains in the world.

Glacier - Giant blocks of ice and snow formed over thousands of years. One single glacier can be the size of an entire city.

Yeti - A mythical furry creature that lives in the Himalaya mountains.

Give them a try!

Hirsute - A fancy word that means "very hairy or furry."

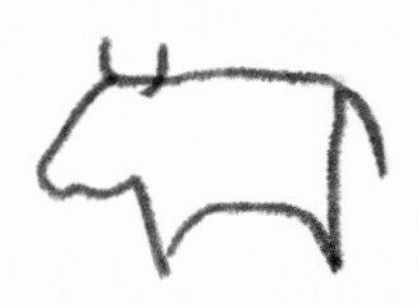

Bovine - A funny word that means something that is like a cow.

Yak - A very furry, cow-like animal from the Himalayas. You might even call it a "hirsute bovine". Give it a try!

Deep in the Himalayas,

beyond small mountain villages and snow-filled valleys...

Across glacial fields and through dangerous icefalls...

Up jagged cliffs, where the air is thin and the
temperature is always freezing....

There lives a yeti.
Alone.

It's true, the Himalayas are remote and the journey is hard, so yetis don't get many visitors or have anyone with whom to make friends. That's just the way it is up there.

However, this yeti is special. She has all the qualities to be a great friend: she is kind and patient, thoughtful and funny, and a really great storyteller (just ask her to tell the one about Melvin and the two yaks).

But the way up to her hut is long and difficult, so she never gets to tell that story...

Though she has dozens of fun games,
she never has anyone to play with.

And although she makes the best
guacamole, she always has
to eat the whole bowl herself.

And though she's a pretty good sax player,
it isn't much fun to play in a band of one.

The Yeti is sure she'd be a great friend, if only she had the chance.
And she knows there's someone out there destined to be her friend.
All they need to do is meet...

But the villages down the mountain are much too warm for her thick fur.
So, she just has to wait until someone makes the long trek up to her hut,
and when they do, she wants to be ready.

Every morning she lights the stove
because she knows that the best thing
after a cold journey is a warm room.

And she prepares hot cocoa
because hot cocoa is the perfect
treat after a long journey in the snow.

She makes the guest bed and fluffs each pillow
so that they are extra soft.

And she gets out all her board games,
even the ones she doesn't particularly like,
because maybe her guest will like those best.

And she organizes all her movies
(she really likes classic sci-fi films)
and makes a big bowl of buttery
popcorn for her guest to enjoy.

She sets up her speaker and plugs in
a microphone for karaoke time.

And of course, she gets her sax ready too.

And she sets the table, puts out chips,
and makes her famous Yeti Guacamole.

And she cooks a big meal,
with both a meat and a
vegetarian option, just in case
her guest has different tastes.

And then she waits...

and waits...

and waits...

But no one shows up.

When it gets late and the Yeti gets sleepy, she lets out a long sigh,
"I guess today is not the day."

So she eats the big meal,
alone, both the regular
and the vegetarian dishes.

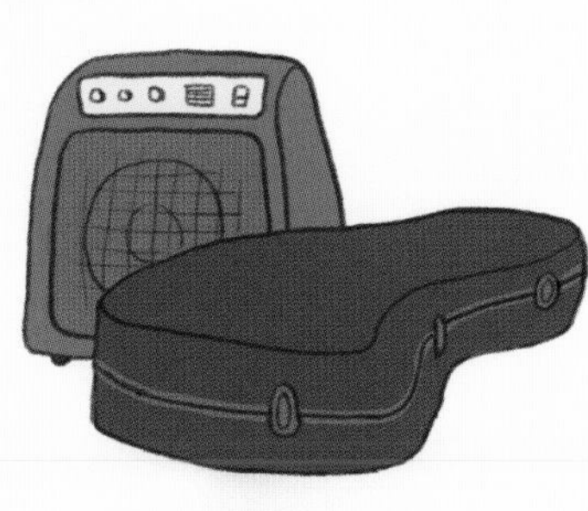

And she packs up her saxophone
and unplugs the microphone.

She puts the movies away and
dumps the bowl of buttery popcorn...

And she packs up all the board games...

And she strips the guest bed
and folds the sheets...

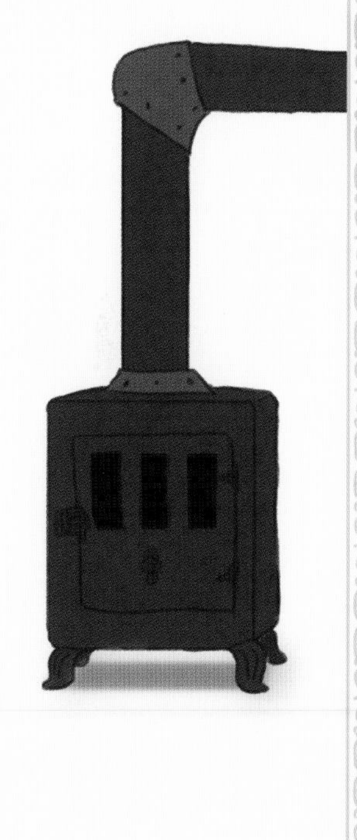

And she drinks the last bit of cocoa
as she puts out the fire.

Then she goes off to bed...

...and hopes tomorrow might be different.

And when she wakes up bright and early the next day, she gets to work as she always does:

She builds a fire and prepares hot cocoa, again.

And she makes the guest bed and fluffs the pillows, again.

And she gets out all her board games, again.

And she organizes her movies and makes a big bowl of buttery popcorn, again.

And she gets out her sax and sets up the karaoke system, again.

And she sets the table and puts out chips and guacamole, again.

And she cooks a big meal – two options – again.

And then she waits, again...

But no one shows up.

Sometimes she thinks,

"What if no one ever comes?

What if there's no one out there to be my friend?"

"What if yetis like me are just destined to live life alone...?"

But she remembers yetis aren’t always alone
because she thinks of Melvin and the two yaks.

And then she laughs. She can’t help it
– that story is too funny not to be told!

And you know what? Her yeti
guacamole is way too good not to be shared.
She plays sax too well to be in a band of one.

She’s not going to just give up!

This yeti has faith that there is
a friend out there somewhere.

And when they show up,
she will be prepared.

So if you like guacamole...

And hot cocoa...

And board games...

And karaoke...

And movies with buttery popcorn...

And funny stories about hirsute bovine...

And if you can travel to the Himalayas...

If you're willing to hike beyond small mountain villages

If you're able to cross the glacial fields and dangerous icefalls...

If you can climb steep jagged cliffs where the air is thin...

And the temperature is always freezing...

And if you want to be her friend...

...the Yeti is ready.